Roary's Birthday Surprise

HarperCollins *Children's Books*

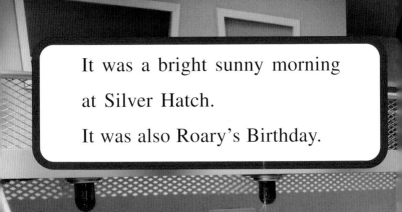

It was a bright sunny morning at Silver Hatch.

It was also Roary's Birthday.

Roary was very happy.

It was his first birthday
at Silver Hatch
and Roary could not wait
to see all of his friends.

"I'll go and see Big Chris first,"
Roary said.

"Morning, Roary," Big Chris said.

He was busy working on Maxi.

"How are you today?"

6

"I'm really happy!" Roary said.

"Why is that, son?"

asked Big Chris.

Roary could not believe it.

Big Chris had forgotten his birthday!

Next, Roary went to visit Cici.

She would not forget his birthday.

The little pink car
was doing her laps.

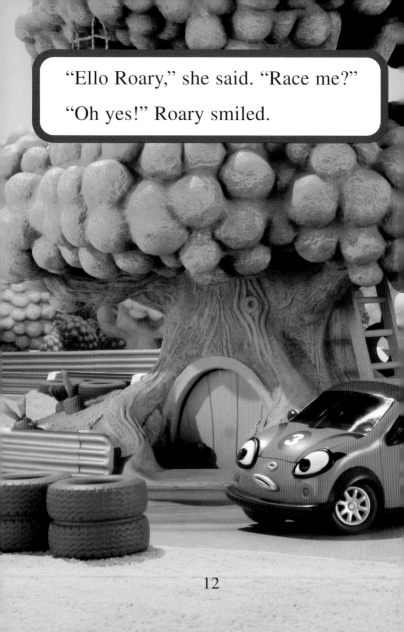

"Ello Roary," she said. "Race me?"

"Oh yes!" Roary smiled.

The two little cars
sped around the track.
Roary tried his best
but Cici was just too fast!

13

"I thought you might let me win today," Roary said.

"Why?" Cici asked.

"Is today important?"

Not Cici as well!

Had everyone forgotten his birthday?

15

Roary drove away sadly.
"Maybe Flash has remembered
my birthday," he thought.

"Hey, Roary!" Flash was sitting outside his burrow.

"Are you excited?" Said Flash

"I knew you wouldn't forget!"
Roary said. He was very happy.

Roary was so upset.
All of his friends had
forgotten his birthday.

"Come on, Roary," Flash said.

"Let's go and see Big Chris.

You need new tyres."

Roary followed Flash

back to the garage.

Roary could not believe it.

All of his friends were there!

"Happy birthday, Roary!"

everyone said.

Cici gave Roary a birthday hat.

"Blow out your candles
and make a wish," Flash said.